BIG BULLY AND M-ME

This hOle book belongs to

_____

More hOle books from Duckbill

BIG BULLY AND
M-ME

Arti Sonthalia

Illustrated by Sebin Simon

duckbill

An imprint of Penguin Random House

DUCKBILL BOOKS

USA | Canada | UK | Ireland | Australia
New Zealand | India | South Africa | China

Duckbill Books is part of the Penguin Random House group of companies
whose addresses can be found at global.penguinrandomhouse.com

Published by Penguin Random House India Pvt. Ltd.
4th Floor, Capital Tower 1, MG Road,
Gurugram 122 002, Haryana, India

First published by Duckbill Books 2015
Text copyright © Arti Sonthalia 2015
Illustrations copyright © Sebin Simon 2015

This edition published in Duckbill Books by Penguin Random House India 2020

Arti Sonthalia asserts the moral right to be identified
as the author of this work

This is a work of fiction. Names, characters, places and incidents are either the
product of the author's imagination or are used fictitiously, and any resemblance to
any actual person, living or dead, events or locales is entirely coincidental.

ISBN 9789383331215

Typeset by PrePSol Enterprises Pvt. Ltd
Printed at Replika Press Pvt. Ltd, India

www.penguin.co.in

MIGHTY MOUSE

My name is Krishna. But if you want to be my friend then you've got to call me Krish without the Na!

I don't like long names because they take too much time to say.

'Divide yourselves into two teams and we'll have a basketball match.'

The coach's whistle went FWEEEEEEEEEEEEEEE!

For a few, very few nanoseconds, I turned deaf.

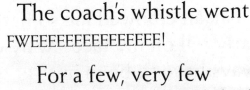

'Ishaan and Green, choose your teams and begin playing.'

The whistle went off again, but this time I stood far away from the coach.

Green is a frizzy-brown-haired boy and he is my First Best Friend. I know Green is a weird name but Green's parents belong to the Green movement. Daddy told me that those who believe in the Green movement spend extra time worrying about protecting the environment.

I waited for Green to call my name. We have been together from first grade and share our tiffins every day on the way back home.

Green and Ishaan began picking out their teams.

Ishaan elbowed me so hard that I nearly fell on my face. 'Why do you always have to be in my way, Krishna?'

Ishaan is the tallest, meanest bully in the world and calls me Krishna, not Krish, so he is not my friend.

Since I am the shortest, skinniest boy in class, I knew Ishaan would never ever choose me, but Green is my best friend, and he always picks me.

Green and Ishaan took turns calling out names for their teams. Green chose Khushi, the-happy-to-do-everything girl and also his Second Best Friend. Ishaan chose this long-nosed girl named Devish.

I waited for Green to call me, but he kept calling other names. I decided I was not sharing my tiffin with Green today.

Now only Randeep—the funny-looking boy—and I were left. Randeep giggled, but I didn't find anything funny.

Green probably didn't choose me because in the last match I tripped over the ball and Randeep tripped over me and then Green over him and Ishaan's team shot a basket. But that didn't mean that I would trip every time!

Finally, Green said, 'Krish.'

I made an angry face at him.

The match began. I managed to get the ball in my hand once, but I couldn't see anything because Ishaan the Big Bully stood right over me.

Before I could think of crawling under him, he snatched the ball and said, 'Shorty, this game is not for you.' He pushed the ball into the basket and stuck his tongue out at me.

I didn't care what Ishaan the Big Bully said, because I was going to be like

Mighty Mouse, who was one of the short players on the NBA basketball team. He won most of the matches for them.

A million something and six was the final score. It's pretty easy to guess who lost—WE!

Green was very upset. I tried cheering him up but he still looked as if he would never play basketball again in a zillion trillion years.

BUMPY ME

When we reached class, we were both glad to see our class teacher Mr Dennis Fergusson. We call him Dennis the Menace, and when he is around something fun always happens.

When everyone had settled down, Dennis the Menace smiled at the class and said, 'When I say GO I want all of you to run with me.' He yelled like a drill officer, 'GO.'

The whole class started running round the chairs, round the tables, with Dennis the Menace leading.

He called, 'STOP.' We stopped. 'GO.' We went round and round again, like a washing machine.

Green and I enjoyed the spin. Dennis the Menace was one of the wackiest teachers we had ever had.

Dennis the Menace said, 'We all know Bright Side School has a show every semester.'

I knew these shows very well. They

involved a lot of talking. Ugghh!!

He smiled. 'This year we are going to do an extempore for the show.'

Randeep asked, 'What's an extempore?'

Ishaan the Big Bully raised his hand and said, 'An extempore is a speech without preparation.'

Big Bully always wanted to answer everything!!

Dennis the Menace nodded. 'An extempore is when you are given a topic on the spot with a limited time to speak.'

I raised my hand. Usually I never ask questions but this was something serious, very serious.

'S-s-sir why d-d-do we need t-t-to do an ex-ex-extempore sp-s-s-s-speech?'

Ishaan the Big Bully tee-heed at my bumpy words and Devish, the long-nosed girl, smirked. Her parents should have named her DeviLish instead of Devish! I hate both of them!

Yes, I stammer.

Every time I open my mouth, my words break and jerk, making it difficult for others to understand what I say. Sometimes the words get stuck in my throat and won't come out.

I stammer at home, I stammer at school, I stammer everywhere.

'Krish, the extempore is going to help you learn to speak in public,' Dennis the Menace said.

We had read-aloud time in which

we were reading out LOUD publicly to the class. Wasn't that enough?

In Grade One in our read-aloud time, we were reading *The Three Little Pigs*.

When it was my turn ,I got stuck on, 'The w-w-wolf huffed and p-p-pu …'

And Ishaan yelled from behind, 'Puffed!' and everyone laughed.

After that wherever I went Ishaan 'Puffed' me. He Puffed me on the way to school, in class, in the canteen, in the bathroom. He even Puffed me in my dreams.

I thought of telling my big brother Bheem but I realised Bheem would only Puff Ishaan harder and when Bheem was not there I would be Puffed back and maybe even blown away.

But I am smarter than Big Bully. Now

whenever we have read-aloud time, I calculate my turn and go to the bathroom.

Dennis the Menace continued, 'Since extempore is a new form of speech for you, it would be a good idea to work in pairs, so that you can help each other.'

Everyone clapped.

It was a great idea, but not for me. I was never ever going to take part in this show. I hoped parents were not invited or else Mom would make sure I participated.

In our Grade Two semester show we did a play of the story *Puss in Boots*. Mom made sure I took part.

I had to wear a hat and had four words to say: 'The prince has arrived.' But when it was my turn, I got stuck and even forgot my hat.

Mrs Omni prompted me from behind. Ishaan, who was the prince, stomped his foot again and again from backstage.

Since Green was Puss in Boots, he even crawled on stage and meowed around me, but I just stood still!

Finally, Mrs Omni announced the arrival of the prince from backstage.

Mom was happy I was on stage. But I made up my mind that even in a zillion trillion years I would never participate in these insane things again.

Why couldn't teachers come up with shows like who can sleep longer, who digs out more mud or who counts more stars?

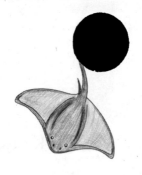

EXPLOSION

Dennis the Menace went on about the extempore. But my mind Puffed away all that he was saying.

'And, the most important part. The pair that does well gets tickets to visit the new aquarium park with their families,' he said.

'Wow!' said DeviLish.

'Whoa!' said Randeep.

'Whoa! Whoa! Whoa!' said everybody.

Everyone's face lit up.
None of us had been there yet.

'Mr Dennis, could we please choose our partners?' Khushi asked.

'I am sorry, Khushi, but I have already made the pairs. Khushi, you are partners with Randeep.'

Khushi's excitement vanished.

I crossed my fingers, hoping Green would be my partner, so that when I didn't turn up for the show he could cover up for me.

'Ambi and Susan. Green and Devish.'

Oh no! NOW who in the world would my partner be?

I wanted to push my fingers in my ears so that I wouldn't hear my name. I wished a star would fall from the sky and we would all run away just before it crushed the school. Then I could name the star Krish because it saved me.

'Next are Ishaan and Krish.' Everything exploded. Star Krish vanished, too.

Ishaan raised his hand. He waved it as if he were drowning, and needed help.

Dennis the Menace finally looked at him.

'Sir, please change my partner. I don't want to be with Krishna.'

'Its K-k-k-krish,' I said.

'Who would want to be the partner of a stammerer? I'll never get those free tickets to the aquarium,' he grumbled.

'Krish and Ishaan, can you both be quiet? There'll be no changing of partners,' Mr Dennis said firmly. 'We will begin practice now. Ishaan and Krish, you go first today,' he said.

First? I froze.

My pants seemed glued to my chair. If I tried getting up they would tear, and everybody would see my fluorescent orange starry underwear.

Ishaan hit me on the head and walked to the front of the class. The glue left my pants as I nearly fell on the floor.

Green whispered, 'Go, Krish.'

I dragged myself.

'I am going to give each of you a topic. You get three minutes to prepare and three minutes to give your speech.' Mr Dennis took out a buzzer from his bag.

Three minutes of talking!
That was too much time!

'Once you get the topic,
you can write down points,
and your partner can help you
prepare.'

But why speak at all, why not just
write? Why didn't anyone think about
people who stammered??

Dennis the Menace placed a box
on the table. 'Ishaan, pick out a topic
from this box and remember, teamwork
always helps.'

Ishaan pulled out a folded chit and
read it. He quickly wrote down a whole
lot of things. Since he didn't even tell
me his topic, I guess he had forgotten
about teamwork.

Dennis the Menace pressed the
buzzer. 'Okay, now start.'

Ishaan faced the class. 'My name is
Ishaan and my topic is "My Favourite

Sport". My favourite sport is basketball … blah … blah …'

With every word that slipped from Ishaan's mouth I got one second closer to my extempore.

The buzzer went off again. Ishaan's turn was over. Everyone clapped. My heart started to beat faster.

'Okay, Krish, now your turn. Just take it easy. I understand it will be difficult for you but it is important to try,' Dennis the Menace encouraged.

My hands trembled as I picked up a topic from the box.

I read it and scribbled till the buzzer went off.

'Start.' He pressed the buzzer.

I was suddenly thirsty, so thirsty that I couldn't feel any

words in my mouth. I hoped
an earthquake, a tsunami or
something would happen and
we could all run out of the
class.

But nothing happened;
everyone was still there, waiting for Mr
Stammerer to open his mouth.

'My …' I paused. 'My-my-my name
is um-um K-k-krish.' My eyes blinked
continuously. 'My-my-my topic is …'

I looked for help at my scribbled
note. It said, 'Reading doesn't help
you, it only makes you lazy because
you don't play, and all reading and no
playing would make you a dull boy.'

Had I written that? Dennis the
Menace would get very, very angry with
me for saying that.

Ishaan whispered from behind,
'Puffed!' and my legs began to shake.

'I-I-I ...'

But the buzzer sounded.

Dennis the Menace leaned over and spoke softly. 'It's all right, Krish, I am sure if you try, you can do it.'

I trudged back to my seat.

NOT FAIR!

'Sir, are you going to invite our parents for the show?' DeviLish asked.

What a mean girl!

Mr Dennis' eyes lit up. 'Yes, Devish.'

'Wow,' Green exclaimed. I sent Green an angry look. There was nothing WOW about this.

My plans had shattered. Ishaan was my partner and Mom was going to know about the extempore. And if Mom had her way, I would have to make a speech in front of everyone. No, there was nothing WOW about this at all.

When I got home I had an urge to ride my bicycle. But it had been three weeks since I had had a ride.

My yellow cycle was no more yellow—it was reddish brown. The colour of rust. The brakes no more braked and everything made a loud noise except the horn.

And the worst thing in the universe was, everyone in the neighbourhood reached everywhere faster than me. Even Green.

I had been begging Mom for a new bicycle, but she

had said, 'Not now Krish, the budget will get messed up.'

Why did the budget always come up when you needed something? And suddenly it would go down. Was it a see-saw or something?

Mom called from the study, 'How was your day, Krish? Is Bheem back?'

'N-n-no Mom,' I said.

Bheem hadn't gone to school today, he was representing Bright Side School in some genius-like thing called a Spelling Bee.

Just then, 'Mom, Mom I won the competition.' Bheem barged in through the front door.

'Wow!' Mom yelled and she rushed out of the study. 'I am so proud of you.' She hugged Bheem. 'You surely deserve the PSP you've been waiting for.'

'Thanks, Mom,' he said.

What happened to the budget, now?

I was happy for Bheem, but I wanted a new cycle badly.

'G-g-great job Bheem,' I said and gave him a high five.

'Let's all go for dinner tonight to celebrate. I'll tell Daddy,' Mom said.

Since Mom was in a good mood, I could mention my new bicycle during dinner.

We were about to leave for dinner when the phone began to ring.

'Krish, could you see who it is?' she yelled from inside her room.

I hated taking phone calls; it took me forever to talk. I waited for Bheem to pick it. But Mom yelled again, 'Krish!'

'H-h-hello,' I said.

'Hi Krish, this is Dennis. I would like to speak to your mom.'

'S-s-s-sir M-mom ...' And before I could tell him she was out of town or down with 110 degrees fever and that no one would be coming for the extempore ...

Mom came up from behind.

'Who is it, Krish?'

'Umm-ummm-umm.'

She took the phone from me and had a long conversation with Dennis the Menace.

'Hey Krish, you didn't tell me about the extempore?' Mom asked.

'I-I-I-I ...'

'I am so glad both Bheem and you are learning new things.'

But I didn't want to learn anything new! Right now I needed a bicycle more than I needed to learn anything new.

THE DEAL

'What would you like?' The waiter asked me.

'D-d-d-d-'

'Double cheese pizza,' Bheem completed.

Throughout dinner, Mom, Dad and Bheem talked about the competition and Bheem's PSP.

'Mom c-c-could you get me a n-n-new bicycle?' I asked, once the dessert arrived.

'Sure Krish. But …'

Dad often said that when Mom stopped on a *BUT* he was going to get one of those things called heart attacks—I wondered if I was going to get one of those things too.

'Let's put it this way. If you perform well in your extempore, I'll get you exactly what you want,' she said.

My mouth fell open.
Extempore vs bicycle!

This was worse than the
heart attack!

'W-w-why
can't I JUST get
m-m-my bicycle?'
I was angry with
Mom for putting
down this silly
condition.

'Krish, your mom and I understand
it's difficult for you, but it is important
to try,' Dad said.

And before I could tell Dad that they
were *not understanding*, Mom said, 'I am
sure Krish will try, and he'll try harder
because he wants the bike.'

This was not fair. But no one said
anything after that, which meant the deal
was sealed for a zillion trillion years.

It was Tuesday morning, and I still

couldn't figure out what to do about Mom's thoughtless DEAL.

I heard Mom's footsteps outside my bedroom. I jumped out of bed and ran straight to the bathroom. I held my stomach and started to throw up.

Mom opened the bathroom door. 'Krish, what's wrong with you? Oh my goodness, you look sick. I'd better not send you to school today.'

Bheem poked his head in. 'Aren't you going to school today?'

'No, he's been throwing up and he looks so pale.' Mom did all the talking for me.

'He looks just fine to me. He's faking it.' Bheem glared at me.

'I-I-am n-not.'

'Are.'

'N-not.'

Mom shoved Bheem out of the bathroom. 'Stop being mean to your brother,' she scolded.

'Take some rest, Krish.' She smiled.

I crossed my fingers. Maybe, just maybe, Mom would change her mind about the bicycle.

In the evening, when I heard Mom's footsteps, I quickly changed into my sick mode again.

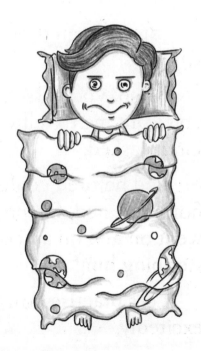

Mom felt my forehead. 'You look good to me now. If you start tomorrow you can get enough practice for the extempore. It's going to help you become a better speaker.'

I didn't want to become anything. All I wanted was a new bicycle.

'W-w-what about my b-b-bicycle, Mom?'

'Krish, a deal is a deal, and I am sure a little trying would do you no harm.' She patted my shoulder and went out.

So there was no changing her mind.

Later, Green dropped in with Khushi.

'Krish, you missed practice today. Do you want me to tell you what we did?' Green asked.

And before I could tell him I was not interested, Green started off. He went on and on and on … there was no stopping him!

'Let's practise now?' Khushi asked excitedly.

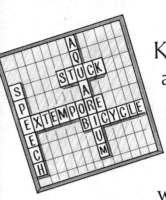

I bumped off Khushi's idea and quickly took out my Scrabble.

Green made the word 'EXTEMPORE'.

Khushi spelled out 'AQUARIUM'.

I made 'STUCK'.

Greem made 'SPEECH'.

I arranged 'BICYCLE'.

I realised we had all gone nuts over the extempore.

No one thought of my bicycle.

After some time, we played in the backyard and for a while, all of us forgot about the extempore.

'Were you really sick today?' Khushi asked.

I felt like telling her I *was* sick of thinking of Mom's deal. But how did

33

Khushi guess I wasn't really sick? Was she a wizard?

After some cookies and milk, Green and Khushi left.

TOO MUCH PRACTICE

The next day at school, I couldn't focus in maths class.

'Where is your mind today, Krish? You've got all your calculations wrong,' Dennis the Menace said.

My mind was busy trying to invent a formula to get my bicycle without doing the extempore.

At lunch break, Green and Khushi loaded their plates with spaghetti. I loaded my plate with nothing.

'Aren't you hungry?' Khushi asked.

'N-n-no.'

'Nervous?'

This girl had to be a wizard!

I mean, she guessed I was not sick. She was the one to figure out that I went to the bathroom whenever we had read-aloud time. It was Khushi who had discovered that I missed all oral tests. And now she knew I was nervous.

My best friend Green
didn't know anything. Green
and I only played, played and
played. We never talked about
my stammering.

Back in class after the lunch
break, Dennis the Menace made us do
a few jumping jacks, and then practice
began.

It was Khushi and Randeep's turn
first. Khushi tried helping Randeep but
he just giggled.

Next, it was Ambi and the shy girl,
Susan. Ambi was fuming at the shy
girl for being shy. She was so angry
that when it was her turn to speak she
fumbled and stumbled. She was to talk
about vehicles. She paused on, 'My dad's
car starts with T…'

Randeep jumped out of his chair and
yelled in his loudest voice, 'But my dad's
car starts with petrol not with TEA!'

I nearly fell off my chair at Randeep's silly joke.

 'Quiet!' Dennis the Menace said.

It was finally Ishaan's and my turn.

This time we did do some teamwork—I wrote for Big Bully but he didn't say anything that I wrote. And when it was my turn, Ishaan wrote for me too.

In big block letters, he wrote, 'PUFFED!'

On Thursday, Ishaan said, 'I don't want a loser to be my partner. Those free aquarium tickets will never be mine.'

'LOSER K-k-krishna,' he mimicked me when Dennis the Menace's back was turned.

For once, Ishaan was right.

I was a LOSER. I was
losing everywhere. I lost
in basketball because I was
short, I was useless at extempore
because I stammered! I would never
get those aquarium tickets and I was
nowhere close to getting my bicycle.

'It's okay, Krish, you can try again.'
Green tried to stop me from being
grumpy. But I knew I would never ever
be able to do this in a zillion trillion
years.

LOSER

In the evening, I went to Green's house.

If I had my cycle I could just zoom past Ishaan's house. Big Bully lived only two houses away from Green.

'Aren't you excited about the extempore?' Green asked, as soon as he saw me.

'N-n-no.' See, I told you—Green just didn't understand anything, though he was my best friend.

'I am super excited, especially about the aquarium tickets.'

I thought of Mom's deal. I hadn't even told Green about it and I was not planning to.

'We have one more day; let's practise?'

Green had to be crazy to suggest something so stupid! I glared at him, 'L-l-let's play.'

His face immediately lit up. We played our favourite pirate game and ended it with a water fight in his backyard.

I was walking past Big Bully's house on my way home, when I heard, 'Puff.'

I felt the hair stand up on the back of my neck. I wished I had my bicycle NOW.

Ishaan stepped out from behind a tree. 'Hey K-k-krishna, let's play a game of football. Or do you want to practise your speech?'

 If I didn't agree he would tell everyone I was scared of him. I decided it would be better to play football.

We started playing on the road outside his house, and each time I tackled Ishaan and got the ball, he pushed me and threw me down.

'Play a game with me, you idiot.'

I looked around to see who had spoken, and saw a tall boy coming out the front door of Ishaan's house. He looked like an older version of Ishaan. He pointed at me and said, 'He is a weakling. I'll give you a real fight.'

When they began to play, the older boy pushed Ishaan just the way he had pushed me, only harder. Each time Ishaan yelled, the older boy laughed and hit him again.

The older boy finally pushed Ishaan down and kicked him. 'You are useless,' he said. Then he went inside.

'W-w-who was th-th-that?' I asked.

'My older brother.' Ishaan looked upset. I had never seen him like this before.

'I guess you'll tell everyone what a wimp I am,' Ishaan mumbled.

For a moment, I thought this would be my chance to get back at him, but instead, I held out my hand to help him up.

'N-n-no Ishaan, I-I-I wouldn't,' I said.

Ishaan looked surprised for a moment.

'Thanks, Krish,' he mumbled.

I smiled. It was the first time he had called me Krish.

As I left, I actually felt sorry for Ishaan. I knew something about him now that was almost as bad as my stammer.

I turned around. Ishaan was still watching me. He waved, and I waved back.

TRY TRY TRY

'What's wrong, Krish?' Khushi asked, the next day during lunch.

Right now, everything seemed wrong. Today was the last day of practice. I didn't want to participate in the extempore and make a fool of myself and if I didn't participate there would be no bicycle!

When we went for swimming class, I had a sudden thought—just as speaking was difficult for me, swimming was difficult for Khushi.

We all knew Khushi was scared of water. She was the only one still swimming with armbands and a tube. But even though Ishaan and DeviLish laughed at her, she hadn't given up!

Why was I so worried about being laughed at?

But then, swimming was not like talking. You didn't have to swim if you didn't want to, but talking was something you had to do if you wanted to get things done.

'Tomorrow is our final day. I want each of you to give your best,' Dennis the Menace announced in class.

He said, 'JUMP.' We jumped. 'STOP.' We stopped. 'JUMP, STOP, JUMP, STOP.' He went on like that for a minute. We all loved Dennis the Menace's quirky ideas. He said it set our minds thinking. Did it? I wondered how.

Randeep started with his speech. He had improved. Even Susan, the shy girl, sounded better.

THOUGHT

JUMP

When it was my turn, I waited for Ishaan to say 'Puff'. But to my surprise, he didn't! Instead, he helped me with the preparation. Was something wrong with him today?

Maybe Dennis the

Menace's jump-stops had set him thinking. Maybe I could try jump-stop with Mom, and she would start thinking about my bicycle.

I opened my mouth to speak, but even though Ishaan was not Puffing me, I was still a little shaky.

'Come on Krish, it's the last day of practice,' Ishaan whispered from behind.

Time was running out. I had to speak up quickly and just when I stuttered out the name of my topic the buzzer went.

Now I was sure that I would never, never get my new bicycle.

Later, Dennis the Menace called for me.

'Krish, I know this is hard for you,' he said. 'I could make it easy by telling you not to participate but I don't want

 you to give up so easily.

'Do you know Hrithik Roshan, the famous Hindi movie star? Even he stammered, but he tried and tried and see how fluently he speaks now.'

Wow, I didn't know Hrithik Roshan stammered. Could I ever be like him?

TOO MUCH
THINKING!!

'Hey Krish, I can't wait for your extempore tomorrow!' Mom said. 'Are you prepared, love?' she touched my shoulder.

I opened my mouth to tell her I wasn't and that please could I get the bicycle anyway, when she said, 'Krish, when I was a kid and was scared I just closed my eyes and said "I can, I can, I can". And you know what? I could.'

I went straight into my room without saying anything and I *set* my mind to think about what Dennis the Menace had said.

But what if someone laughed at me? I thought first.

But Khushi didn't care when people

made fun of her arm-bands
and tube, I thought second.

I thought third of Ishaan.
He did not Puff me, nor did he
make fun of me, yesterday.

I thought fourth, maybe we could be
friends?

Could a bully ever be a friend to
anyone? I thought fifth.

Finally, I decided.

You are not going to believe it in a zillion trillion years, but I actually decided on the sixth thought to speak up and do the extempore! After all, Mom's deal was to *try* and make the speech; it was not to be perfect.

I quickly jumped out of bed and made small notes on different topics that could be in the extempore. If I planned my speech beforehand, I would stutter less.

I thought of the topic, 'My Best Friend'. That would be easy. I knew all about Green.

Then, 'My Favourite Food'. I was aware of all that went into making pasta.

'My Class'—there was lots to tell about Ishaan and DeviLish.

'The Solar System.' I loved everything to do with stars and planets.

My stomach fluttered as I thought of what would happen if I got a topic that I didn't know much about.

'What are you doing?' Bheem asked, walking into my room.

'Pr-pr-preparing for th-the ex-ex-extempore.'

He looked at my notes. 'That looks good. When I was in Grade Three even I had to do it.' Suddenly Bheem looked concerned. 'Will you be able to do this? Are you scared?'

I was. I was very scared.

'During my spelling competition I was very nervous and then there was this one spelling that I just couldn't get. Before leaving Mom had told me, "If you get stuck just say 'I can, I can, I can'." And that's what I did, and I got it!!'

I didn't know Bheem had to try hard to win. I thought he was some kind of a genius who could just do everything without any fear.

Even geniuses got scared? Now that was a new thought!

Suddenly, I felt less nervous.

COMMUNICATION

Everyone in class was shaking hands and wishing one another luck.

Except me! Mine were too wet to shake.

I really shouldn't have got myself into this, but before I could think of running away, or throwing up, or maybe even jumping out of the window, Mom, Dad and Bheem walked into the auditorium with their biggest smiles, as

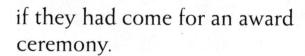

if they had come for an award ceremony.

Soon, all the parents had taken their seats. I spotted Green's parents. His mom wore a green dress and dad a green tie. Green really did have a *green* family.

Ishaan's big-bully brother was there too, but Ishaan looked comfortable.

Dennis the Menace immediately took charge. 'A warm welcome to all the parents. I am sure you are all very eager to see the children perform. We shall begin with the extempore. Randeep and Khushi, you are first.'

Khushi's and Randeep's extempore was great. Randeep was giggly but his speech was good.

Susan was shy. As for Ambi, her topic was 'Your Interests'. She went on and on about dressing up. What a show-off!

My stomach started spinning while Green and DeviLish performed. I wished I could drown myself in a swimming pool and drink all the water.

'Krish and Ishaan, it's your turn now,' Dennis the Menace said.

'Come on, Krish.' Green pushed me.

Ishaan picked up a folded paper and looked puzzled. I peeped to see what it was. 'Solar System.' I quickly wrote down everything I knew.

Ishaan's time began. You are not going to believe this, but Ishaan said everything I had written and also things I didn't know. His speech was the best I had heard.

Now it was my turn.

'Good luck,' Ishaan said.

I smiled and Puffed away all the horrible things about Ishaan from my mind. I was sure now Ishaan would never ever Puff me.

When I read the topic, I thought I was about to faint. Ishaan snatched the paper from me and made notes. But I already knew a lot about this topic.

When you stammer, not even in a zillion trillion years would anyone know the meaning of communication better than you.

I'll tell you why.

You can't order in a restaurant without pointing at pictures. You can't scream or yell for your favourite team. You can't ask your brother his girlfriend's name. Nor can you ask how girls like Khushi are wizards. And why Green's family is so Green!

61

I heard Dennis the Menace whisper, 'Come on Krish, you can do it.'

I closed my eyes and thought of what he had said about Hrithik Roshan.

And if Bheem could manage the scary spelling test with Mom's special 'I can I can I can' mantra, even I could manage this.

So I was going to try too.

I began, 'M-m-my name is K-k-krish and my topic is "C-c-communic-c-cation".'

I squeezed my eyes shut. 'To c-c-communic-cate means to say how you feel, i-i-it is i-i-important to t-talk.

'E-e-even K-k-king George VI d-d-didn't know how t-t-to c-c-comun-i-icate.' Mom had told me about his bumpy-speech movie.

I looked at all the strangers. They didn't seem strange. I kept speaking.

Soon the buzzer went off.

I had spoken a lot for one day. I hadn't spoken so much in a zillion trillion years.

Green and Khushi jumped out of their seats and everyone stood up and clapped for me. I couldn't believe it. I, Krish the stammerer, had managed to complete an extempore.

'I have an announcement to make.'

We all looked at Dennis the Menace.

'Everyone has worked very hard for the show, but one team has put in an extra effort. The aquarium tickets go to …' He paused.

'Krish and Ishaan, for working as a team! And everyone in class gets a special ice-cream cone!' he said excitedly.

I couldn't believe it!

'Yeah! Yippee!!!' everyone screamed.

Ishaan beamed with delight and came running towards me.

He gave me a high five. 'You were good and thanks for the help during my extempore. I am so glad you were my partner.'

'M-m-meee toooo.' Was I saying these words to Ishaan?

Mom hugged me and said, 'My little star, you deserve your new bicycle.'

Bheem grabbed me and gave me one of his crushing hugs and Dad swirled me in the air.

Khushi and Green were so thrilled that they nearly knocked me down.

This was the best day of my life in a zillion trillion years!

Arti Sonthalia has had her work published in a number of books in the *Chicken Soup for the Soul* series. This is her first book for children, and she has loved working on it.

Sebin Simon simply illustrates
his dreams, inspirations and
expressions. From childhood,
the only thing that made
him happy was drawing and
painting, so when he grew up
he chose to be happy.